Nate the Great
STALKS
STUPIDWEED

Nate the Great
STALKS
STUPIDWEED

by Marjorie Weinman Sharmat

illustrated by Marc Simont

A Yearling Book

Published by
Yearling
an imprint of
Random House Children's Books
a division of Random House, Inc.
New York

Text copyright © 1986 by Marjorie Weinman Sharmat
Illustrations copyright © 1986 by Marc Simont
Extra Fun Activities copyright © 2005 by Emily Costello
Extra Fun Activities illustrations copyright © 2005 by Jody Wheeler

The jumping horse design is a registered trademark of Random House, Inc.

Yearling is a registered trademark of Random House, Inc.

Visit us on the Web! www.randomhouse.com/kids

Educators and librarians, for a variety of teaching tools, visit us at
www.randomhouse.com/teachers

ISBN-13: 978-0-440-40150-6
ISBN-10: 0-440-40150-X

Reprinted by arrangement with Delacorte Press
Printed in the United States of America
One Previous Edition
New Yearling edition June 2005
30 29 28 27
UPR

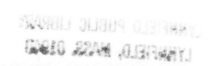

To my son Andrew,
who I'm sure would have given me
his enormously helpful suggestions
even if I didn't do his laundry

I, Nate the great detective,

was weeding my garden.

My dog, Sludge, was digging in it.

Oliver came over.

Oliver always comes over.

Oliver is a pest.

"I have just lost a weed," he said.

"No problem," I said.

"You may have all of mine."

"But this was *my* weed,"

Oliver said. "Can you help me

find it?"

"I, Nate the Great, am not going
to look for a weed.
I only take important cases."
"This is an important weed,"
Oliver said. "I bought it
for a nickel at Rosamond's
ADOPT-A-WEED sale.

Rosamond picks weeds

that nobody wants

and she finds homes for them."

"I believe it," I said.

"She gave me a Certificate of Ownership,"

Oliver said. He pointed to something

sticking out of his back pocket.

It was a thick, rolled-up

piece of paper

with a ribbon tied around it.

Oliver pulled the paper

out of his pocket

and handed it to me.

I untied the ribbon

and unrolled the paper.

It was long.

It had printing on it.

Oliver ....
Owner of Superweed
Superweed. Born Six
Weeks Ago In The Left
Corner of The Vacant Lot
On Oakdale Street

← Rosamond's
Garantee
Your Money Back
If Not Satisfied

There was a shiny seal
stuck on the paper.
It also had printing on it.

"See? It's an important weed,"
Oliver said. "It also came with
a record that Rosamond made
to play to her weeds
to help them grow.
Be proud you're a weed,
wild and free,
and you might grow up
to be a tree."
"Rosamond thinks big," I said,
"as well as strange."
I gave the Certificate of Ownership
back to Oliver.
He put it in his pocket.

"Tell me," I said,

"what happened after you

bought the weed?"

"I took it home,"

Oliver said. "But it looked sick.

I played Rosamond's record for it.

Then it looked sicker.

So I went to the library

and found a big book about weeds.

I took it home.

I read about sick weeds

and healthy weeds.

The book told me how

to make sick weeds healthy.

It gave three steps.

Step One. *Put the weed in dirt.*

I got a pot with dirt in it.

Then I stuck the weed in it.

Step Two. *Give the weed sun*.

I took the weed in the pot

out to my back porch

and put it on my railing

where the sun was shining.

Step Three. *Give the weed water.*
I went into the house
for a glass of water.
When I got back to the porch
with the water,
the pot was there,
but the weed was gone."
"Perhaps the weed did not like
what you were doing to it,"
I said. "Perhaps it escaped."
"I never did the third step,"
Oliver said.

"I have already solved your case,"

I said.

"Today is a breezy day.

The weed blew away in the breeze.

The breeze is going east.

Your weed could be in China by now."

"But China is way outside my porch,"

Oliver said.

"And my porch is screened in."

"I, Nate the Great,

do not want to look for your weed," I said.

"I would not know it

if I found it."

"My weed looks small and scraggly and sick,"

Oliver said.

"It has a yellow bud.

Rosamond said it will grow

into a flower

that will reach

as high as the sky.

That is why I bought it."

Oliver stood there

and looked up at the sky.

He might stay forever

if I did not look for his weed.

"Very well," I said.

"I will take your case."

I wrote a note to my mother.

Dear mother,
I am on a small
scraggly and sick
case. I wish I
weren't. I will be back.
Love,
Nate the Great

"Show me where your weed disappeared,"

I said to Oliver.

Oliver, Sludge, and I walked to

Oliver's back porch.

It was screened in.

I looked for holes and cracks.

But I could not find any.

I looked at the railing.

It was covered with dirt.

A pot of dirt was sitting on it.

Beside the pot was a big book.

With a dirty fingerprint on the cover.

But I could read the cover.

It said *Wonderful Weeds of the World*.

I walked around the porch.

I looked in corners,

and under and on top of things.

Sludge sniffed.

"Your weed has to be

on this porch," I said.

"But it isn't here.

This is a tough case.

I must go to Rosamond's

ADOPT-A-WEED sale.

Perhaps I will learn something there."

"I will follow you," Oliver said.

"Not if I can help it," I said.

I, Nate the Great, and Sludge

ran to Rosamond's house.

She was sitting outside
behind a table
that was covered with weeds and cats.
There was a big can of water
under the table.
There was a sign beside the table.

"I am looking for Oliver's lost weed,"

I said.

"He lost his weed?" Rosamond asked.

"That was my star weed.

It will grow to the sky.

It's Superweed."

"It's sick," I said.

"Oliver didn't love it enough,"

Rosamond said.

"Would you know it

if you saw it again?" I asked.

"I know all my weeds,"

Rosamond said. "I keep a list

of them in this book."

Rosamond opened a book

she had on her lap.

"Oliver's weed has a yellow bud,"
she said.

"I already know that," I said.

"And its name is Superweed,"
Rosamond said.

"I know that too."

I, Nate the Great, had a
better name for it.

But I did not think that
Rosamond would like
Stupidweed.

"You have told me everything
I already knew," I said.

"Oh, good," Rosamond said.

"I knew I could help you."

Rosamond closed her book.

Annie and her dog, Fang,

were coming down the street.

Sludge ducked under the table.

He knocked over the can of water.

It fell on Rosamond's feet.

PLOP!

"Sloppy Sludge!" Rosamond cried.

"You got my feet wet!"

This was not a good day for Sludge.

He was afraid of Fang.

He was also afraid of Rosamond's cats.

I spoke to Annie.

"I am looking for a weed
with a yellow bud on it."

"Maybe Fang ate it," Annie said.

"Is Fang a weed eater?" I asked.

"Fang will eat almost everything,"
Annie said. "Watch!"

Annie shouted, "Fang! WEED!"

Fang grabbed a weed in his teeth
and started to run away.

"You owe me two cents, Fang!"
Rosamond shouted.

Rosamond's four cats ran after Fang.

I hoped that Fang and the cats
would have a big fight.

I hoped they would all lose.

The world would be safe forever.

Sludge ran out
from under the table.
He knew it was time to leave.
We had to look for Stupidweed.
But where?
Perhaps we should look where
lots of things grow.
Perhaps we could find a clue
in the woods
or in a park.

Sludge and I walked to the woods.

We peered inside.

It was dark and scary in there.

It was almost as scary as Fang.

I, Nate the Great, hate cases

where I have to be brave.

Sludge and I crawled into the woods.

We heard something behind us.

It was gaining on us.

It was Oliver.

Sludge and I hid behind a tall tree.

Oliver ran into the woods.

Sludge and I ran out.

We ran to the park.

We sat down on a bench.

Everything was sunny and bright.

And safe.

I liked it there.

Flowers and plants were everywhere.

Was there a clue among

all these growing things?

Was there a weed?

Suddenly I saw something.

It was Claude.

Claude is always losing things.

He was crawling down a path
among the flowers.

"Did you lose something?" I asked.

"A worm," he said. "It crawled
into the ground.

I can't see it
but I know it is in there.

It is right under our noses.

Can you help me find it?"

This was not a good day for
me, Nate the Great.

I had been asked to find a weed.

I had been asked to find a worm.

It was time to do something
important.

I went home and made pancakes.

I gave Sludge a bone.

I thought about the case.

I had to find the weed
and lose Oliver.

But I was stumped.

The weed could not have left
Oliver's porch.

But it was not there.

I thought about clues.

What had I learned?

The weed's name was Superweed.

I knew that was not important.

The weed had a yellow bud.

Maybe that was important.

Maybe it wasn't.

The weed was last seen inside a pot
on Oliver's railing.

Last seen was always important.

What was Oliver doing

just before the weed disappeared?

He was reading from a book

and looking at his weed

and turning away from his weed

to go into his house.

Were *those* clues?

I thought of Rosamond.

She was strange.

That was not a clue.

That was her problem.

Then I thought about her book

and her can of water.

Hmm.

I looked at Sludge

eating his bone.

He always tried to help with my cases.

But all he had done was knock over

Rosamond's can of water.

Was he trying to tell me something?

I thought about Claude
and his worm.
Suddenly I knew I had
a lot of good clues.
I had to go back to Oliver's house.
It was hard to do.

Oliver was sitting on his back porch.

"I lost you in the woods," he said.

"Did you find my weed?"

"I am getting close," I said.

I looked at his railing.

"Where is your weed book?"

"I took it back to the library,"
Oliver said.

"Then I, Nate the Great, must go
to the library."

"I will follow you," Oliver said.

"I know it," I said.

Sludge and I rushed to the library.

Sludge had to wait outside.

I went inside.

I looked for weed books.

I found *Wonderful Weeds of the World*.

It had a dirty fingerprint

on the cover,

so I knew it was Oliver's copy.

I pulled it down.

I opened it up.

I looked inside.

I found what I knew I would find.

Oliver's weed!

It was between two pages.

It was pressed against

Step Three.

It did not look sick anymore.

It looked dead.

I took the weed from the book
and put the book
back on the shelf.
I knew that Steps One, Two,
and Three could not help
Oliver's weed.
Nothing could help Oliver's weed.
I left the library.
Oliver was outside with Sludge.
I held up the weed
with both hands.
It needed both hands
to keep it up.
"Here is your weed," I said.
"The case is solved."
"How did you find it?" Oliver asked.

"Clues," I said. "Lots of clues.
I saw Claude looking for a worm
in the ground.
He said he could not see it

but he knew it was in there

just under our noses.

I thought about that.

Your weed could have been *in*

something close by,

but we still could not see it.

What was near the pot?

What was just under our noses?

Your weed book!

But you gave me the biggest clue

when you said you were using the book

when the weed disappeared.

When I saw your book,

it was closed.

I remember reading the title

on the cover.

It had to be closed

for me to do that.

But it should have been open

because you were still using it.

Rosamond closed *her* book

when she was *through* with it.

Why was your book closed

when you *weren't* through with it?"

Oliver shrugged.

"I, Nate the Great, will tell you why.

The breeze blew it closed

while you were getting the water."

"So what?" Oliver said.

"*After* the weed fell into it!" I said.

"What?" Oliver gasped. "Why would

the weed do that?"

"Because it was hit by the
Certificate of Ownership
sticking out of your back pocket.
When you turned to go into your house,
the certificate hit the weed,
and the weed fell into the book,
and the weed fell into the book.
PLOP!
Just like Rosamond's can of water
fell over when Sludge hit it.

Turn your back to the pot, Oliver."

Oliver turned.

"Aha! Your certificate is aimed

directly at the pot. Perfect aim."

"I wasn't trying," Oliver said.

"Your weed was sick," I said.

"It was in dry dirt.

It was easy for it to plop.

It was right under our noses.

But we couldn't see it.

Just like Claude and his worm."

"So my weed didn't go to China,"

Oliver said.

"I, Nate the Great,

make a few mistakes."

Oliver stared at his weed.

"This weed looks terrible.

It will never reach the sky.

I am going to Rosamond's house

to get my nickel back."

"I am going home," I said.

I said good-bye to Oliver.

I liked doing that.

"I will be over later," he said.

"I know it," I said.

Sludge and I went back to our garden.

I started to weed again.

But I was tired of weeds.

Perhaps Rosamond could come over
and pick them all.

She would give them names
and homes.

That would make everybody happy.

Especially me.

I had better things to do.
I, Nate the Great, went back
to the library
and took out
a good, clean book.

～Extra～
Fun Activities!

What's Inside

Oliver thought Stupidweed was special. Nate went back to the library. He learned that Stupidweed was a dandelion—common but tough. He found out about some other wicked weeds, too.

NATE'S NOTES: Famous Weeds

Dandelions are tough. They grow bright yellow flowers. The flowers turn into globes of feathery seeds. Each one looks like a tiny parachute with a seed passenger. The wind can blow the seeds for miles.

Dandelions grow anywhere they find dirt, sun, and water. They will even grow in sidewalk cracks. If you cut off the leaves, the plant's long root will send up new ones.

Some people say the only way to get rid of dandelions is to _eat_ them. They put the leaves in salad. They make wine from the flowers. You can even eat the root! But be careful. Some people put poison on their lawns. If you want to eat dandelions, grow your own.

Four hundred years ago, Captain John Smith was exploring North America. One thing he found? **Poison ivy.** This weed causes an itchy, oozy rash. Its leaves produce a strong oil. A tiny drop could make 500 people itch. Oil on dead poison ivy plants can cause a rash, too.

Getting rid of poison ivy is hard. Pull the plant up and you'll start itching. Mowing it releases the oil into the air. The same goes for burning the ivy.  Experienced gardeners get rid of the plants by digging them up down to the roots (wearing gloves!) or treating them with chemicals. Kids are smart to stay away.

Giant hogweed is pretty. Along streambeds, it grows as tall as fifteen feet. Its lacy white flowers can be two and a half feet wide. But the weed has a nasty side. Its sap is poisonous. If you get the sap on your skin and then go into the sun, you will get big blisters! One plant can produce 50,000 seeds. They can come up seven years after being released.

Kudzu comes from Japan. People brought it to the United States in the 1890s. They planted it to stop soil from washing onto roads. It worked. It worked too well. In the southern United States, kudzu grows everywhere. With good light and water, it will grow a foot a day. It covers trees. It covers houses. It covers cars. Some people call it the plant that ate the South.

NATE'S NOTES:
Other Weird Plants

Rosamond is strange. So are these plants.

Voodoo lily. This Asian plant looks like a huge purple gourd. It grows a flower that smells like rotting meat. Flies like to lay eggs in rotting meat, so this flower attracts flies. The flies carry off the flower's pollen. Result? More stinky plants!

The **stinking corpse lily** smells even worse than the voodoo lily—because it is much bigger. It flowers only once in a while. When it does, it makes a monster flower. Each one is three feet in diameter and weighs twenty-five pounds. The huge, bumpy orange flower pumps out the smell of rotting flesh. The good news: It grows far away—in the rain forests of Sumatra and Borneo.

The **Venus flytrap** eats flies and other bugs. The plant grows a small "cage." The flytrap's cage looks like a green clam with spiky edges. The plant lures bugs with sweet nectar. A bug crawls into the cage. If it touches a trigger hair inside, the cage will snap shut— trapping the bug inside! Venus flytraps live in North and South Carolina, among other places.

The **ant plant** from Indonesia grows hollow green "pillows." These pillows make comfy homes for ants. The ants move in. The plant sends roots into the pillows.

The roots suck up the ants' poop. Yummy!

Mimosa is also called sensitive plant.
Run your hand over a mimosa's feathery
leaves and they close up. If you keep
touching it, the entire branch will droop to
the ground. Why? The plant may be trying
to make animals think it looks yucky.
Anything to avoid being eaten. The
mimosa comes from Brazil, but people have
planted it everywhere. It's fun to own
plants that do tricks.

How to Make Seaweed Salad

Weeds grow in the sea as well as on land. People collect them and dry them. Buy some seaweed at an Asian food market. Then make a salad!

GET TOGETHER:

- 3/4 ounce of dried seaweed (wakame, hajiki, and arame are good)
- 3 tablespoons rice vinegar
- 3 tablespoons soy sauce
- 2 tablespoons sesame oil
- 1 teaspoon sugar
- 1 teaspoon grated ginger
- 1/2 teaspoon garlic, chopped up
- 1 tablespoon toasted sesame seeds

MAKE YOUR SALAD:

1. Put the dried seaweed in a bowl. Cover with water. Let soak 5 minutes.
2. Stir together the vinegar, soy sauce, oil, sugar, ginger, and garlic. This is your salad dressing.
3. Drain the seaweed.
4. Toss the seaweed with the dressing.
5. Top with the sesame seeds.
6. Enjoy!

How to Grow a Monster with Green Hair

You want to grow something. Here's a fun project to try.

GET TOGETHER:

- colored felt-tip markers
- a Styrofoam cup
- a knee-high nylon stocking
- potting soil
- alfalfa seeds*
- a mister or a spray bottle
  filled with water

* You can buy these at a health-food store

MAKE YOUR GREEN-HAIRED MONSTER:

1. Use the markers to draw scary eyes, a nose, and a mouth on the cup.
2. Fill the stocking with potting soil until it is about the size of an orange.
3. Tightly knot the stocking. Place it in the cup. It should look like the top of your monster's head.
4. Sprinkle the "head" with seeds.
5. Place on a sunny windowsill. Mist lightly every morning for two or three days. Watch your monster grow "hair"!

How to Make Worms on Toast

Worms help weeds—and other plants—grow. They loosen up the soil and recycle nutrients. What great things could they do inside your stomach?

Makes one serving. Ask an adult to help you with this recipe.

GET TOGETHER:

- one hot dog
- a plastic knife
- a pot of boiling water
- a slice of bread
- ketchup

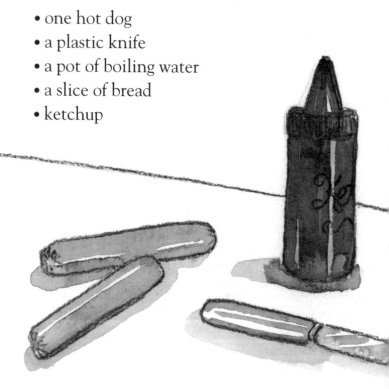

MAKE YOUR WORMS ON TOAST:

1. Slice your hot dog into about six worm-shaped strips.
2. Place the slices in the pot of boiling water. Cook over medium heat. (Or microwave at 50% power for about 2 minutes.) The dogs are done when they curl up like worms.
3. Toast your bread.
4. Put your hot dog worms on the toast. Squirt on some ketchup.
5. Eat! Enjoy!

How to Turn a White Flower Red

Impress your friends with this cool trick.

GET TOGETHER:

- scissors
- one or more white carnations*
- a plastic cup
- water
- red food coloring

* This trick will not work as well with other types of flowers—but you can try!

TURN THE WHITE FLOWER RED:

1. Use the scissors to trim half an inch off the bottom of the flower stem. Be careful! Scissors are sharp.
2. Fill the cup halfway with water.
3. Drop in some food coloring. Make the water fairly dark.
4. Place the flower in the colored water.
5. Wait a few days. You will see the flower slowly turn red.

How to Press Garden Stuff

Oliver pressed Stupidweed by mistake. Some people press flowers and other things from the garden for fun. Here's how to try it.

Ask an adult to help you with this.

STEP ONE: GO COLLECTING

1. Grab a paper bag. Then head outside for a mini nature hike.
2. Pick up some stuff to press. Good things include wildflowers, weeds, leaves, grasses, seeds, and dead bugs.
3. In spring, look for dandelions and clover. In summer, try Queen Anne's lace and wild strawberries.
4. In autumn, find colorful leaves and small pinecones.
5. In winter, pick up twigs from evergreen trees and holly bushes. Can you find a dead moth or bee?

STEP TWO: GIVE IT A SQUEEZE

1. Take what you found and make it flat.

GET TOGETHER:

- the stuff you collected in STEP ONE
- a roll of waxed paper
- two heavy books, such as phone books or encyclopedias

*Be careful!
Live insects sting. Some plants can give you a rash. Don't touch anything unless an adult says it's safe. Never pick a flower someone has planted without asking. Angry gardeners can be dangerous.*

21

DO THE SQUEEZE:

1. Place the stuff you collected on a piece of waxed paper.
2. Cover with a second sheet of waxed paper.
3. Place the waxed paper "sandwich" between the two heavy books.
4. Wait a week.
5. Take out your pressed stuff.

STEP THREE: MAKE SOMETHING

1. Glue pressed flowers onto heavy paper to make birthday cards.
2. Squish pressed insects between sheets of contact paper to make bug bookmarks.
3. Make a leaf collage for your teacher.
4. Imagine your own project. Do it!

Happy

Birthday

Library Riddles

Q: What building in town has the most stories?

A: The library!

Knock knock!
Who's there?
Rita.
Rita who?
Rita lot of good books!

Q: How many librarians does it take to screw in a lightbulb?

A: I don't know. But I know where you can look it up!

Q: Where does a librarian sleep?
A: Between the covers!

Q: Why did the librarian slip?
A: She was in the nonfriction section.

Q: What did the detective do when he didn't believe the librarian's story?
A: He booked her!

Q: What's a book's favorite food?
A: Bookworms on toast!

Q: What is the astronaut's favorite part of the computer?
A: The space bar!

Go on a Library Treasure Hunt

Nate found Oliver's weed in the library. What can you find at your library? Here are some ideas to get you started.

Can you find the **children's room**?
What is the name of the **librarian** who works there? Can you discover one interesting thing about him or her?

Find three **storybooks** you'd like to read. Does the library have any NATE books you haven't read?

Find three **nonfiction books** that look good. Can you find any books about weeds or plants?

Find a **magazine** that looks interesting.

Does your library lend **videos** or **DVDs**? Look for one you've never watched before.

Does your library have a **cozy place** to read? Try a few of the chairs. Pick your favorite.

Does the library have **a space** where people hold meetings or performances? Are there any upcoming events that sound like fun?

Where are the **restrooms**?

Does your library have a **copy machine**? How much does it cost to make one copy?

Is there a **computer** for kids? Can you surf the Internet on it? Try it out!

Do you have a **library card**? If not, ask the librarian how to get one. That way you can take home books and other library stuff.

Have you helped solve all Nate the Great's mysteries?

❑ **Nate the Great**: Meet Nate, the great detective, and join him as he uses incredible sleuthing skills to solve his first big case.

❑ **Nate the Great Goes Undercover**: Who— or what—is raiding Oliver's trash every night? Nate bravely hides out in his friend's garbage can to catch the smelly crook.

❑ **Nate the Great and the Lost List**: Nate loves pancakes, but who ever heard of cats eating them? Is a strange recipe at the heart of this mystery?

❑ **Nate the Great and the Phony Clue**: Against ferocious cats, hostile adversaries, and a sly phony clue, Nate struggles to prove that he's still the greatest detective.

❑ **Nate the Great and the Sticky Case**: Nate is stuck with his stickiest case yet as he hunts for his friend Claude's valuable stegosaurus stamp.

❑ **Nate the Great and the Missing Key**: Nate isn't afraid to look anywhere—even under the nose of his friend's ferocious dog, Fang—to solve the case of the missing key.

❏ **Nate the Great and the Snowy Trail**: Nate has his work cut out for him when his friend Rosamond loses the birthday present she was going to give him. How can he find the present when Rosamond won't even tell him what it is?

❏ **Nate the Great and the Fishy Prize**: The trophy for the Smartest Pet Contest has disappeared! Will Sludge, Nate's clue-sniffing dog, help solve the case and prove he's worthy of the prize?

❏ **Nate the Great Stalks Stupidweed**: When his friend Oliver loses his special plant, Nate searches high and low. Who knew a little weed could be so tricky?

❏ **Nate the Great and the Boring Beach Bag**: It's no relaxing day at the beach for Nate and his trusty dog, Sludge, as they search through sand and surf for signs of a missing beach bag.

❏ **Nate the Great Goes Down in the Dumps**: Nate discovers that the only way to clean up this case is to visit the town dump. Detective work can sure get dirty!

❏ **Nate the Great and the Halloween Hunt**: It's Halloween, but Nate isn't trick-or-treating for candy. Can any of the witches, pirates, and robots he meets help him find a missing cat?

❏ **Nate the Great and the Musical Note**: Nate is used to looking for clues, not listening for them! When he gets caught in the middle of a musical riddle, can he hear his way out?

- **Nate the Great and the Stolen Base**: It's not easy to track down a stolen base, and Nate's hunt leads him to some strange places before he finds himself at bat once more.

- **Nate the Great and the Pillowcase**: When a pillowcase goes missing, Nate must venture into the dead of night to search for clues. Everyone sleeps easier knowing Nate the Great is on the case!

- **Nate the Great and the Mushy Valentine**: Nate hates mushy stuff. But when someone leaves a big heart taped to Sludge's doghouse, Nate must help his favorite pooch discover his secret admirer.

- **Nate the Great and the Tardy Tortoise**: Where did the mysterious green tortoise in Nate's yard come from? Nate needs all his patience to follow this slow . . . slow . . . clue.

- **Nate the Great and the Crunchy Christmas**: It's Christmas, and Fang, Annie's scary dog, is not feeling jolly. Can Nate find Fang's crunchy Christmas mail before Fang crunches on *him*?

- **Nate the Great Saves the King of Sweden**: Can Nate solve his *first-ever* international case without leaving his own neighborhood?

- **Nate the Great and Me: The Case of the Fleeing Fang**: A surprise Happy Detective Day party is great fun for Nate until his friend's dog disappears! Help Nate track down the missing pooch, and learn all the tricks of the trade in a special fun section for aspiring detectives.

❑ **Nate the Great and the Monster Mess**: Nate loves his mother's deliciously spooky Monster Cookies, but the recipe has vanished! This is one case Nate and his growling stomach can't afford to lose.

❑ **Nate the Great, San Francisco Detective**: Nate visits his cousin Olivia Sharp in the big city, but it's no vacation. Can he find a lost joke book in time to save the world?

❑ **Nate the Great and the Big Sniff**: Nate depends on his dog, Sludge, to help him solve all his cases. But Nate is on his own this time, because Sludge has disappeared! Can Nate solve the case and recover his canine buddy?

❑ **Nate the Great on the Owl Express**: Nate boards a train to guard Hoot, his cousin Olivia Sharp's pet owl. Then Hoot vanishes! Can Nate find out *whooo* took the feathered creature?